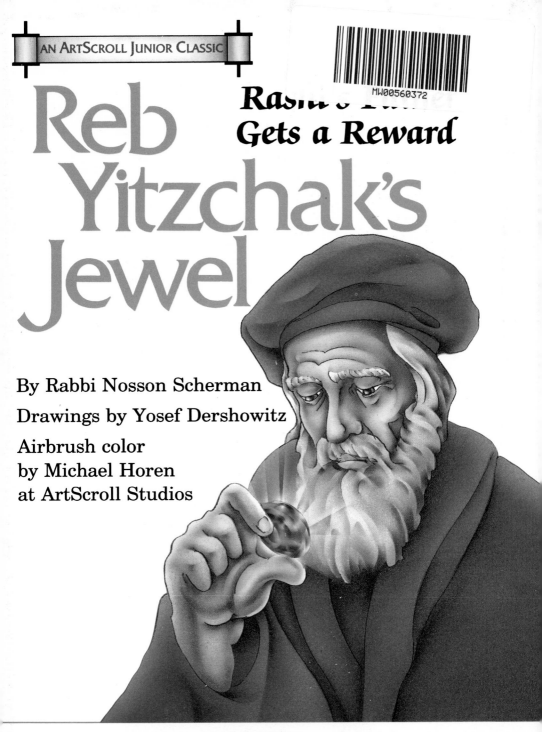

Reb Yitzchak's Jewel

Rashi's ~~Little~~ Gets a Reward

By Rabbi Nosson Scherman

Drawings by Yosef Dershowitz

Airbrush color
by Michael Horen
at ArtScroll Studios

© Copyright 1988, by MESORAH PUBLICATIONS, Ltd.
1969 Coney Island Avenue / Brooklyn, N.Y. 11223 / (718) 339-1700
Produced by SEFERCRAFT, INC. / Brooklyn, N.Y.

Reb Yitzchak and his wife lived in the French city of Troyes. They were both very good Jews. But one thing made them both very sad.

They did not have children.

Reb Yitzchak made a living selling jewels
to very rich men. His nicest jewel was a big,
blue sapphire.

Reb Yitzchak told his wife, "If we can sell
the sapphire, we will be able to help poor
people with the money. But I feel so bad that
we do not have children to spend the money
on."

One day a stranger from a faraway city
came to Reb Yitzchak's house. He said, "My
master is the King. He sent me to buy your
sapphire. He wants to use it as an eye for his
idol."

"Here! I will give you a thousand gold coins for your stone."

Reb Yitzchak did not want his nice sapphire to be in an idol. He said, "I don't want to sell the sapphire!"

The man said, "My king will give you *two* thousand gold pieces. Even *three* thousand!"

Reb Yitzchak said, "I don't care how much money you want to pay. I don't want to sell."

The man was very angry. "I warn you. The king will send soldiers to kill you. He wants the sapphire!"

Reb Yitzchak was afraid. Quickly he thought of a plan. He said, "All right. I will sell it to the king. I will go with you and bring it to the king myself."

He wrapped up the sapphire and put it in his pocket. He packed his *tallis* and *tefillin* and some kosher food.

Reb Yitzchak and the man traveled to the river. They got on a boat to sail to the king's palace.

Reb Yitzchak said, "Do you see the sun? My sapphire is as bright as the sun. Do you see the water? My stone is bluer than the water. No one has ever seen such a beautiful stone!" This was part of his plan.

"Please let me see the stone!" said the man.

Reb Yitzchak said, "No, I cannot show it to you. What if you lose it?"

"I promise you I will take good care of it," the man said. The more Reb Yitzchak said no, the more the man begged him.

Finally Reb Yitzchak said, "All right, I will show it to you. Come with me."

They walked over to the side of the boat. Reb Yitzchak looked this way. He looked that way. He made sure no one was watching. Then he reached into his pocket and took out a tiny package. He opened it and gave the sapphire to the man.

The man took the stone and held it in his hands. The sun's rays shone on the sapphire. It looked like fire. It sparkled. It was so beautiful that the man's eyes opened wide.

He said, "Aaah, Reb Yitzchak. You were right. Never has there been such a sapphire. It is more beautiful than the eyes of my king's idol. He will give you a big reward for it. You will be rich!"

"Please be careful," said Reb Yitzchak. "Don't let anything happen to it. Now give it back to me."

The man said, "Reb Yitzchak, I want to thank you for letting me see it and hold it. Here it is."

Reb Yitzchak held out his hand and the man handed him the sapphire. Just then, Reb Yitzchak lost his balance and almost fell.

He dropped the sapphire. It fell into the river!

"No. No," screamed Reb Yitzchak. "My sapphire is lost. My beautiful jewel is gone. What will I do. Oooh!"

With that, Reb Yitzchak fell down in a faint.

People crowded around and asked what happened. The man told them. Everyone felt sorry for Reb Yitzchak. They poured water on his face and he woke up. He began to cry. He felt so bad that he could not even stand up!

Finally the people helped him stand up. He looked at the water. He was very sad.

The king's man was sad, too. He said, "What will we tell the king? He will be very angry."

Soon the boat came to shore and all the people got off.

The man took Reb Yitzchak to the king and told him what happened. The king was very angry. He shouted at the man, "Why did you ask to see the sapphire?"

He shouted at Reb Yitzchak,
"Why did you show it to him?"

Reb Yitzchak cried and cried. He cried so much that the king felt sorry for him. The king said, "I will not give you money for the sapphire that you lost. But I will give you money to buy some food and get back home."

On the way back home, Reb Yitzchak did not cry. He had lost a valuable jewel, but he didn't care. He and his wife would always be happy that their sapphire did not become part of an idol.

When he got back home, there was an old man waiting for him. It was Eliyahu the Prophet.

Eliyahu said, "Reb Yitzchak, Hashem knows that you dropped the sapphire on purpose so it should not be the idol's eye."

"Hashem is very proud of you and your wife because you are such good people. Hashem will bless you with something that is worth more than thousands of gold coins. You will have a son whose Torah will light up the whole world!"

The next year, Reb Yitzchak and his wife had a baby boy. They named him Shlomo. When Shlomo grew up, he wanted to help all the Jews know the Torah better. He wrote comments to explain all the hard parts of the Torah.

People saw what he wrote. They said, "This is so good! Who wrote it?"

Others answered, "This was written by Rabbi Shlomo Yitzchaki. We call him RASHI."

Now, all Jews study Torah with *Rashi*. His words make the Torah sparkle even more than the sun.

The pages of the Talmud and Midrash, and the chapters of our history are filled with beautiful stories about our great leaders and ordinary good people.

In the **ArtScroll Junior Classics**, we bring you these stories, written for young boys and girls. They are illustrated with beautiful pictures that everyone will love.

We are sure that parents and teachers — and mostly children — will love these books. They tell stories that everyone should know, and tell them in a way that everyone will enjoy.